Mother Goose
Book of Rhymes

As Told and Pictured By
MARGARET EVANS PRICE

MMVIII ◆ GREEN TIGER PRESS

Tom, Tom, the piper's son

TOM, TOM, the piper's son,
Stole a pig, and away he run.
The pig was eat, and TOM was beat,
And TOM went howling down the street.

Jack and Jill

JACK AND JILL
went up the hill
To fetch a pail of water.
JACK fell down and broke his crown,
and JILL came tumbling after.

Rock-a-bye Baby

Rock-a-bye-baby,
    on the tree top,
When the wind blows,
    the cradle will rock.
When the bough breaks,
    the cradle will fall,
And down will come baby, cradle and all.

Little
Miss
Netticoat

LITTLE Miss Netticoat, in a white petticoat,
With a red rose,
The longer she stands,
The shorter she grows.

Goosey Gander

GOOSEY, Goosey, Gander,
whither do you wander?
Upstairs, and downstairs,
and in my lady's chamber.
There I met an old man
who wouldn't say his prayers.
I took him by the left leg,
and threw him
down stairs.

Mary, Mary, Quite Contrary

MARY, Mary, quite contrary,
    How does your garden grow?
With Silver Bells and cockle shells,
    And pretty maids all in a row?

LITTLE Bo-Peep has lost her sheep,
And can't tell where to find them.
Leave them alone, and they'll come home,
Wagging their tails behind them.

The Queen of Hearts

THE Queen of Hearts,
  She made some tarts,
  All on a summer's day.
The knave of hearts, he stole those tarts,
  And with them ran away.

Three Blind Mice

THREE blind mice,
   see how they run,
They all ran after
         the farmer's wife.
She cut off their tails
         with the carving knife,
You never saw such a sight
      in your life,
As three blind mice.

Simple Simon

SIMPLE SIMON met a pieman,
Going to the fair,
Said Simple Simon to the pieman,
"Let me taste your ware."

SAID the pieman to Simple Simon,
"Show me first your penny."
Said Simple Simon to the pieman,
"Indeed, I haven't any."

Little Tommy Tucker

LITTLE Tommy Tucker sings for his supper,
What shall he have but white bread and butter?
How shall he cut it, without any knife?
How shall he be married without any wife?

SEE, SAW, Margery Daw,
Jenny shall have a new master.
She shall have but a penny a day,
Because she can't work any faster.

GEORGIE Porgie, puddin' an' pie,
Kissed the girls and made them cry.
When the girls began to play,
Georgie Porgie ran away.

GREEN TIGER PRESS

COPYRIGHT © 2007, BLUE LANTERN STUDIO

ISBN 13 978-1-59583-134-7

THIS PRODUCT CONFORMS TO CPSIA 2008

FOURTH PRINTING PRINTED IN CHINA ALL RIGHTS RESERVED

THIS IS A REPRINT OF A BOOK FIRST PUBLISHED BY THE STECHER LITHO COMPANY IN 1917

LAUGHING ELEPHANT BOOKS

3645 INTERLAKE AVENUE NORTH SEATTLE, WA 98103

WWW.LAUGHINGELEPHANT.COM